Feeling SHY!

First published in 2017 by Wayland

Text copyright © Wayland 2017
Illustrations copyright © Mike Gordon 2017

Wayland
Carmelite House
50 Victoria Embankment
London EC4Y 0DZ

Wayland Australia
Level 17/207 Kent Street
Sydney, NSW 2000

Managing editor: Victoria Brooker
Creative design: Paul Cherrill

ISBN: 978 1 5263 0079 9

Printed in China

FSC
www.fsc.org

MIX
Paper from
responsible sources
FSC® C104740

Wayland is a division of
Hachette Children's Books,
an Hachette UK company.
www.hachette.co.uk

Feeling SHY!

Written by
Kay Barnham

Illustrated by
Mike Gordon

WAYLAND

The new girl had been at school for three hours and she *still* hadn't said a word.

At break time, she stood in the corner of the playground and kept her eyes on her shoes.

Daisy decided that it was
time to take action.

"I'm Daisy," said Daisy to the new girl. "What's your name?"

"I'm Isla," whispered the girl, kicking a stone. "It's my first day and I feel really shy. Everyone's got loads of friends and I don't know *anyone*."

"I'll be your friend," said Daisy brightly.
"Would you like to come for a play date after school tomorrow?"
Isla smiled. "OK," she said.

The next day, Daisy had a surprise for Isla —
she'd invited two more girls to the play date ...
Isla's cheeks glowed red. "H-h-hello,"
she said nervously.

Daisy bit her lip. Had she done the wrong thing?
Would Isla be furious?

But she needn't have worried. Everyone was so friendly that Isla was soon laughing and smiling.

When it was time to go, she hugged Daisy. "Thank you," she said. "Now I have *three* new friends."

On Saturday, it was Olivia's birthday. Daisy had been looking forward to her friend's party for weeks. It was going to be so much fun.

It was fun. They played musical statues and pass the parcel. Daisy even won a prize!

But then she noticed that someone was *not* having a good time.

Daisy's friend Isaac was staring out
of the window, ignoring everyone.
"Hey, what's up?" said Daisy, nudging him.

"Nothing," mumbled Isaac. "I didn't want to come to this stupid party anyway. Party games are for kids."

"I see," said Daisy. But she didn't believe him. She wondered if Isaac was actually a bit shy. Maybe that's why he wasn't joining in.

The next game was a three-legged race.
"Will you be my partner, Isaac?" asked Daisy.
"If I have to," grumbled Isaac.

After a few minutes, Isaac was laughing as hard
as everyone else. He started talking to some
of the other children. And when he won a prize,
he wore the biggest smile at the party.

The next morning, Mum was super
busy cleaning the house, while Dad cooked
Sunday lunch.

"What's going on?" said Daisy, dodging the
vacuum cleaner.

16

"You've forgotten that Auntie Myrtle and Uncle Don are visiting?" gasped Mum. "Quick, go and tidy your room. And tell your sister to do the same. I want the house to be *spotless*."

Auntie Myrtle and Uncle Don arrived in
a flurry of hugs and kisses.
  "Haven't you grown!" Auntie Myrtle said to Daisy.
"Er, yes," said Daisy.

"So where's your little sister?"
boomed Uncle Don. "Has she grown too?"
There was a squeak from behind the sofa.
"Come out, Poppy!" said Mum. "Stop being silly."
But Poppy didn't appear.

19

Daisy crept behind the sofa.
"What's wrong?" she asked Poppy.

"I feel shy," muttered her little sister.
"If I come out, everyone will make a fuss."
"They'll make more of a fuss if
you're hiding," Daisy said.

"Hmm," said Poppy, thinking for a moment.
"I suppose so." So she took a deep breath.
"Surprise!" she said, bravely jumping up.
"There you are!" said Uncle Don.
"Haven't you grown!" added Auntie Myrtle.
"Now, when's lunch? I'm starving."

The next week, Daisy discovered for herself
what it was like to feel shy, when she visited
the badminton club for the very first time.

"Don't worry,"
said Dad, when
he dropped her off.
"You love badminton.
It'll be great!"

Daisy wasn't too sure about that.
"Bye, Dad," she said, pushing
open the door to the
sports hall.

THWACK! THWACK! THWACK! THWACK!
Shuttlecocks flew backwards and forwards.
Players leapt to and fro. All around, club
members talked and laughed.

Daisy gulped. This was terrifying.
There were so many people here and she didn't
know *any* of them. What was she going to do?
She felt too shy to say a single word.

"IS EVERYTHING ALL RIGHT?"
bellowed a coach from the other end of the club.
Suddenly, everyone was staring at Daisy.
Oh dear. Now she felt shyer than ever.

Then Daisy remembered how she'd helped others to beat their shyness. Hmm.

Could she perhaps follow her own advice ...?

So Daisy took a deep breath and went to speak to the coach. In a flash, she'd joined in with a game of badminton. And before she knew it, she'd made new friends.

Daisy smiled as she whacked a shuttlecock.
Feeling shy wasn't fun. But making friends
was the best feeling in the world.

FURTHER INFORMATION

THINGS TO DO

1. Did you know that shy people are sometimes called wallflowers, because they stand back against the wall instead of joining in? How many wallflowers can you make friends with this week? You might help them to stop feeling shy.

2. Which is your favourite shy character in this book? Draw a picture of them looking super-confident instead!

3. Make a colourful word cloud! Start with 'shy', then add any other words this makes you think of. Write them all down using different coloured pens. More important words should be bigger, less important words smaller.
Start like this...

SHY
hiding behind the sofa

nervous

NOTES FOR PARENTS AND TEACHERS

The aim of this book is to help children think about their feelings in an enjoyable, interactive way. Encourage them to have fun pointing to the illustrations, making sounds and acting, too. Here are more specific ideas for getting more out of the book:

1. Encourage children to talk about their own feelings, if they feel comfortable doing so, either while you are reading the book or afterwards. Here are some conversation prompts to try:

What makes you feel shy?
How do you stop feeling shy when this happens?

2. Make a facemask that shows a shy expression.

3. Put on a feelings play! Ask groups of children to act out the different scenarios in the book. The children could use their facemasks to show when they are shy in the play.

4. Hold a jealous-face competition. Who can look the MOST shy?! Strictly no laughing allowed!

BOOKS TO SHARE

A Book of Feelings by Amanda McCardie,
illustrated by Salvatore Rubbino
(Walker, 2016)

Giraffes Can't Dance
by Giles Andreae, illustrated by Guy Parker-Rees
(Orchard Books, 1999)

Miss Hazeltine's Home for Shy and Fearful Cats
by Alicia Potter, illustrated by Birgitta Sif
(Walker, 2016)

Dinosaurs Have Feelings, Too: Sophie Shyosaurus
by Brian Moses, illustrated by Mike Gordon
(Wayland, 2015)

The Great Big Book of Feelings
by Mary Hoffman, illustrated by Ros Asquith
(Frances Lincoln, 2016)

Two Shy Pandas
by Julia Jarman, illustrated by Susan Varley
(Andersen Press, 2013)

READ ALL THE BOOKS
IN THIS SERIES:

Feeling Angry!
ISBN: 978 1 5263 0015 7

Feeling Frightened!
ISBN: 978 1 5263 0077 5

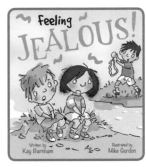

Feeling Jealous!
ISBN: 978 1 5263 0075 1

Feeling Sad!
ISBN: 978 1 5263 0071 3

Feeling Shy!
ISBN: 978 1 5263 0079 9

Feeling Worried!
ISBN: 978 1 5263 0073 7